DARA Ó CONAOLA was born on the Aran Islands' Inis Meáin but lives now on the neighbouring island, Inis Oírr. Widely acclaimed as a writer of short stories, he has also written a novella, stories for children, biographies, and has a deep interest in local history and lore. Dara's senses are finely tuned, his imagination fertile, and the world he creates in his short stories one of wonder and of awe.

GABRIEL ROSENSTOCK is regarded as the most versatile and prolific writer and translator of his generation. He is a former Chairman of Poetry Ireland / Éigse Éireann, a member of the Irish Writers' Union, the Society of Irish Playwrights, the British Haiku Society, the Haiku Society of America, and is an Honorary Life Member of the Irish Translators' Association.

NIGHT RUCTIONS

Dara Ó Conaola

NIGHT RUCTIONS

Selected Short Stories

by

DARA Ó CONAOLA

Translated from the Irish
by
GABRIEL ROSENSTOCK

Cló Iar-Chonnachta
Indreabhán
Conamara

First edition 1990
Second edition 1999

Translations © Cló Iar-Chonnachta
Introduction © Cló Iar-Chonnachta
Original stories © Dara Ó Conaola

Illustrations by Peter Donnelly

ISBN 1 900693 15 1

Cló Iar-Chonnachta receives financial assistance from The Arts Council

Publisher: Cló Iar-Chonnachta, Indreabhán, Conamara
     Tel: +353 91 593307   Fax: +353 91 593362   e-mail: cic@iol.ie
Printing: Clódóirí Lurgan, Indreabhán, Conamara
     Tel: 091 593251 / 593157

Contents

Other books by the same author:

An Gaiscíoch Beag
An Gúm 1979

Mo Chathair Ghríobháin
An Gúm 1981

Cor in Aghaidh an Chaim
Ceardshiopa Inis Oírr Teo 1983

Guide to the Aran Islands
Cuairt ar Oileáin Árann
Published annually since 1978

Thatched Homes of the Aran Islands
An Teachín Ceanntuí
Ceardshiopa Inis Oírr Teo 1988

Amuigh Liom Féin
Ceardshiopa Inis Oírr Teo 1988

Misiún ar Muir
Ceardshiopa Inis Oírr Teo 1992

Saothar Albert Power
Ceardshiopa Inis Oírr Teo 1996

Between Worlds

Translator's Preface by Gabriel Rosenstock

Dara Ó Conaola was born in Inishmaan (Inis Meáin), the middle island, and now lives on the smallest of the three islands, Inisheer (Inis Oírr), where he works as a teacher, managing a craft shop in the summer months and taking to the pen when the urge is too strong — the urge to break the silence and the urge to entertain. Ó Conaola is one of the last writers in Irish to inherit the secret of the *seanchaí*, or traditional storyteller, an art-form perfected in Ireland to such a degree that today we boast the greatest archive of traditional lore in Europe. However, Ó Conaola is no mere dresser-up of long forgotten tales. He is not, essentially, a folklorist but a living exemplar of the traditional artist in transition stage, a writer of superb narrative charm, caught — but not uncomfortably — between the old world and the new.

Like his fellow Aran-islander, Liam O' Flaherty, Dara Ó Conaola has the unique ability in many of his stories to appeal to adult and older child alike.

Being an islander, his senses are awake to every movement of wind, every stirring of wave, light and half-light. His perceptions pierce further than mere acute observations of natural phenomena, of the animal and vegetable kingdom. His peerings into the other world are shamanistic voyages, not the product of a powerful and child-like imagination, but that of a sensibility strangely in tune with primordial factors long since smoked out by the march of progress through Western Europe.

Here is a short-story writer, then, whose art is as old and as bewitching as St. Elmo's Fire on the waves, as old as man's fear of himself and the otherworld, and yet an art that is buoyantly and reinvigoratingly new. A naive artist in some respects, perhaps, we often find him talking to himself and yet conscious that someone is listening.

In *Night Ructions*, first published bilingually in an Irish-American bilingual journal, The Bridge, we follow the sheep, a little aimlessly at first, along the winding, stony roads of Aran, then tension mounts and fills the air: two rams confront each other in the dead of night. The chiaroscuro effect of sheep, night and the moon is extremely simple and yet exceedingly effective.

Ó Conaola is the author of *An Gaiscíoch Beag*, a classic tale for children about a boy nick-named cynically 'The Little Warrior', because he was a lazy, feckless good for nothing — until the time comes for his initiation into the world of manly deeds. This classic has been available now for over a decade and still awaits translation! In a world of mass-media onslaught and sensationalism, where human beings grow up as minions to consumerism, sitting numbed in front of the TV, safe in the knowledge that the burglar and smoke alarms are in working order, in a world where nature groans through her dying forests and lifeless waterways, Dara Ó Conaola lives on and writes on, in the oldest literary vernacular in North Western Europe, on a small island where it seems nothing and everything is happening at the same time, giving us sentences that are sculpted as simply and naturally as the stones of Aran, a world in which reality, frequently harsh, is relieved and redeemed by the balm of the word.

Introduction

I have often heard it said that island life is conducive to writing. There are long lists of island writers, or writers who were inspired by island life, in the annals of the two literatures. One thinks immediately of J.M. Synge who discovered some subtle spiritual quality in Aran that had previously eluded him. I was born and reared in the Aran Islands. I left, though later returned. They called me back. It wasn't the subtle magic sensed by Synge that drew me back, though I was aware of that too. It was something more. In Irish we call it *dúchas,* the ineluctable native experience, the compound of tradition, place and language. I would like my children to know that *dúchas* and that of Ireland in general. The pounding of storm waves on wintry nights, the wild sound-effects from the chimney accompanying the wonder-tales that have been handed down through generations of story-tellers; or a lambent spring day when the earth seems to move and the heart leaps in your chest.

When I was growing up in Aran most people hadn't even a radio, so, naturally enough, we relied on traditional forms of entertainment. We were just as happy. Nothing could please us more than sitting around the fire listening to my father telling old stories. Before long we came to know them ourselves. "Tell us about the giants!" we'd say. And he'd be off. Any change at all, any attempt at an edited or watered-down version late at night and we'd stop him in his tracks. "That's not how you told it the last time!" Story telling thrilled my imagination and as soon as I learned to read I got my hands on books. From reading, it was only one more step to writing.

A weekly Irish-language paper, *Amárach,* published a story of mine when I was only twelve. A dog talking about himself! I'm still barking away, not up the wrong tree I hope, and articles, poetry and stories flow from my pen in an even, steady stream. *An Gúm,* educational and general publishers, published two books of mine: *An Gaiscíoch Beag,* a retelling of a mock-heroic tale and *Mo Chathair Ghríobháin,* a collection of stories. More books of mine have been published since then.

Usually I'm reluctant to discuss my own writing since, in my opinion, every piece of writing should speak for itself. However, every author and poet has ideas about his work. I write from my own experience, people and places I know, and there is nothing I like better than adding my own imagination to a traditional tale and coming up with a new story entirely.

Old cottages inspire me always. They remind me of the people who lived in them long ago. Indeed, I find the environment of my family house a great source of inspiration. For example, in the first story, the house would seem to have a life of its own, and nothing in it, great or small, is without significance.

Dara Ó Conaola

Spider

Every morning I smoke a pipeful before getting out of bed. It's an old habit of mine. It does me some kind of good that I can't explain. It may be no more than a peculiarity that has stuck to me, though it may just as likely be a subconscious strategy to acquire the peace of mind I need. Call it my matins, if you will.

I sit up in bed. I put on my bawneen. I take the pipe that's sitting next to me. Then the tobacco. I cut it. I rub it. I redden it at my ease. All thoughts of the world leave my head as I contemplate the night's adventures, sleep — which they say is a brother of Death — my worldly duties, and the day ahead.

During these morning meditations of mine, I sometimes shudder at the thought of being disturbed. It would be calamitous to intrude; not only would my reveries be interrupted, my whole day would be ruined and my plans all in a tumble.

The people of the house have learned not to interfere with me and I usually manage a very restful meditation. And then I get up, full of eagerness to tackle whatever bit of work I have laid out for myself.

That's the way it was one morning recently. My mind was gently drifting as usual, my back to the gable, facing the little cupboard and the small chimney; it was then I noticed something that got my wind up.

A big slob of a spider it was, dangling from the beam and he measuring up the prospects of crashlanding on the cupboard.

"Well, you big oaf you," says I. "What business have you to be disturbing the likes of me?" Basically, you see, I'm a peevish, liverish type, mornings especially. Consequently, my first impluse was to teach this impudent lout a lesson. Ah, wasn't he the lucky fellow I wasn't

1

reclining a bit nearer him.

After a few puffs of the pipe, the evil drained from me and soon I was back enjoying my reveries once more and me boyo, the spider, spinning away like mad in my mind's attic.

For all I know, I thought, the fellow could be my poor deceased grandfather, or even my grandmother, or some other relation sent back to earth to spin more karmic web. There's no knowing, I said to myself.

Whoever he was, he was making precious little progress, oscillating to and fro, this way and that, and coming no nearer the cupboard.

I left him to his fate. Let him spin his own destiny, I said in my own mind, for I am not obliged to help or hinder him.

I spent an eternity watching him. To and fro. This way and that. When he tired of his gyrations, by which stage I was near gaga myself from watching him, up he goes. Up his thread, straight up to the beam. He vanished in the darkness.

Then I thought of the day ahead, the work and the foostering that awaited me. I put aside the pipe and readied myself to get up... but I wasn't ready yet with the spider.

Whatever innocent glance escaped the corner of my eye what was it I saw but himself coming down the wall; his gait had the resoluteness of a penitent pilgrim. He was making for the cupboard.

Down he came. He reached the top of the cupboard but he didn't stop there. Down still further. He reached the board under the cupboard. He walked the plank. Where the devil are you off to? He seemed to know well enough.

There was a little hole that had escaped my notice until now on the left side of the cupboard, low down, just between the frame and the wall. In he goes.

It was a great relief to me that he stayed there. I got up. I must admit I was very content with the way the morning reveries had progressed.

Many is the morning since then I have watched his peregrinations, up and down, up and up, until eventually he would end up in his little dust bowl between board and wall. He gave me no further cause for annoyance and in the end I grew attached to him. For all I know, as I have previously mused, he may be one of the dear departed.

Time flies. Things change. Things grow. Things flourish. The world moulds people and things, at no time more conspicuously than in spring. The days stretch. Dark winter memories fade.

This is the time when new resolves to be good burgeon in the heart and one attempts to tackle life with something of the zest of a crusader. My wife had such an attack recently, or so her symptoms would suggest.

"Now," says she, "now that spring is here, hadn't I better clean out that room and slap a coat of paint on it — it's an anathema, that's what it is, a holy show altogether."

I had no objection to this move. Indeed, I'm partial to spruceness myself.

She scoured. She painted. It wasn't long before she reached the cupboard. Then I remembered my eight-legged friend. "Look," says she, "would you look at that confusion of webs!"

I closed my eyes, foreseeing the nemesis. When I opened them again, the boards and joints were wiped clean. The spider's dwelling razed, the tenant evicted.

I said nothing. I accepted it — mistakenly or otherwise, I shall never know — as dharma.

Of late, mornings seldom slip by that I don't say a little prayer for the dead. It's not that I give unequivocal credence to what may have been no more than a fanciful notion crossing my mind when he first crawled into my life; not at all. But just in case, and, as I have ventured to opine, there's no knowing.

Love and Salt

My mother was a very patient woman when I was young in Ireland long ago. I never minded her at all. I'd never do anything but what suited myself best. I was one dreadful rapscallion.

My mother had no one else but myself and I was a pet as well as being a bit of a fool. My poor father was gone a long time. I never set eyes on him.

We were poor, terribly poor. But we were quite happy. I hadn't much worries anyway. My mother, of course, did all the work.

I was willing to do one thing. I used to be out on the side of the hill keeping the cow we had out of the big dangerous holes. I liked that job. At the same time I used to be hunting rabbits, as a past time.

It was the old dog we had that used to do the hunting for me. To be precise, he did most of the herding too. He was as wily as an old cat. Alert too. Many a time but for him the cow would have plunged over the cliff.

One evening I was about my usual business on the hillside. The dog was half a mile away where he had noticed the cow in some danger. As luck would have it what do you think scampered between my legs but this whopper of a rabbit. Bless us and save us — and the dog a half a mile away!

What had I on my shoulder but a sickle. The rabbit was in no hurry, seeing no dog about. He got my blood up. I took a swipe at him with the sickle. And got him on the back. I had him stretched cold. "Now," said I to him, "that's stopped your gallivanting".

I set to thinking then that it was a powerful deed I had done. I was more than a bit surprised. I had no idea I was half as good.

What came in to my mind was that I could take off and go anywhere now. It wasn't a bad man who could slay a mountain animal with one blow. I can boast of that

5

forever.

I went home fairly swelled with pride. I had the rabbit. And my dog by my side. And the cow ahead of me ready to put in her stall. My mother was overjoyed to see the rabbit. We'd have it for dinner the day after. "Musha," says she, "that old dog is worth his weight in gold. It's hardly a day he doesn't bring home the sauce."

"Maybe," says I, "but it wasn't him but me that did the deed today. I killed this rabbit. I hit it with the sickle while he was off half a mile away."

"Better still," says she.

"I'm thinking," I said, "that I'm as good as any man — that it's time I went out into the world."

"What are you saying at all?" she asked. "What do you mean?"

"What I'm saying," says I "is that it's time I left the Glen and go trapsing the world in search of my fortune."

"Musha, and where would you be off to my poor man!" says she. "The likes of you never left the Glen. Sure you wouldn't last three days out there on your own, may God look down on your head."

"That's how it is now, mother. When I struck that rabbit today I began to think about myself. I've a mind to go off."

"Indeed don't go," says she," but stay here with me. Stay another while at least."

"There's no point in your going on about it," says I. "You'd better prepare some provisions for the road because I'll be off tomorrow at the break of day."

And we left it at that.

The following day I was up at the crack. My mother stuffed three loaves of bread in my satchel for the road. She was sorrowful and heartbroken. The only shilling in the house she put in the satchel as well.

"Don't fret at all about me," says I, "because however long it takes me to return it's not a shilling I'll have in the satchel but shillings galore."

"May God guide you," says she, weeping.

I too was lonely going, leaving my native home behind me, the first time in my life. It pained me greatly to leave my mother alone. But there was nothing else I could do at the time.

But I had hope as well. And courage. Wasn't I a man of valour? I proved that yesterday on the hill. And I strode forth valiantly. I was wandering on and on until dew and eveningtide, and the dung beetle was going behind the dock leaf.

By the time I had arrived at a crossroads I had no notion under heaven which way I should go. If I went one way it might lead to my downfall. Which way would lead to good fortune? That was no easy question to answer.

Thus it was for a long while as I scratched my head. Thinking and poring over my lot. "Hello! Hello!"

Suddenly I heard this little voice behind me. It fairly surprised me. I looked around to see who it might be. I had to look well because it wasn't easy to see him. Then I did.

A small grey man. He wasn't anything like my size, and I wasn't big. He had a green coat and a hat on.

"God be with you," says he approaching me.

"God and Mary with you," says I just as boldly.

"You'd think," says he, "that you were someone in a bit of a quandary," says he, "the way you're scratching your crown."

"That would be correct," says I. "I have a great difficulty to resolve. A great difficulty."

"And what might be the nature of this difficulty?" asked the grey little man. And indeed didn't I tell him.

"It's like this," I says, "I'm standing here this good while like some idiot not knowing from God which road of all the roads he's made would be better for me to take. And that is the nature of my quandary."

"Quite problematical," says the little grey man, "but not insuperable, if you follow me."

"How's that now? Can you tell me the right road to take?"

"Never mind for a moment," says the grey little man, winking at me like a rogue.

"Listen," says he, "have you any money on you? Or did your mother give you anything when you left home?"

"Sure I've nothing at all — but the last shilling that my mother had in the house, and that she gave me with the goodness of her heart."

"Would you give me the shilling?"

"And leave me with nothing, like God's poor?"

"What good is your shilling now and you not knowing from God above which way to go? Look at me," says he, "standing here all the while without a penny or a ha'penny, looking for help. I'm telling you, if you'd give me that shilling I'd be eternally grateful to you. "

Didn't I take pity on him in the end. My heart softened and I parted with the last shilling my mother had left in the house.

He was more than grateful, and why wouldn't he?

"Come here," says he, "concerning this quandary of yours as to which way you should go. Now if you take my advice you'll go this way," pointing his hand, "and when you go up the road a bit you'll come to a house. A farmer's house," says he, "and when the farmer asks you what you're after, you tell him it's work you want, that you'd heard about him."

He receded then, into the darkness. I didn't see him again. But I didn't spend long peering after him. I went off taking the route he had said.

It wasn't long before I reached a house. The little man had spoken true. It was a farmer's house. I knocked on the door. A girl came out.

"I'd like to see the master," says I.

She went in and before long she was back again.

"What business have you with him?" she asked.

"I must speak with the master," says I.

She went in again. Soon she was back once more.

"Go in so," says she.

She brought me into a posh parlour. The farmer sat at

the fire like a lord without shoe or stocking, his two feet stretched out to the fire. He turned around.

"And what would you be wanting boy?" says he, "at this unlikely hour?"

"I heard," says I, "that you're looking for a servant-boy."

"And who told you that?"

'Oh," says I, bold as bedamned, "I heard it going past me."

'That's the best way," says he. "I'll give you work if you're able and lots of it. Are you any good," says he then, "at herding cows and sheep?"

"None better," says I.

And it was no lie. Hadn't I spent my whole life up to now at it.

"Now," says he, "I'd better tell you about your pay. I'll make the same arrangment with you as I've made with every servant boy up till now. If you don't like it you needn't bother and you can head off somewhere else. Do you understand that now?"

"I do, sir," says I.

"The arrangement I'll make with you is this, that you work for me a year and a day. I'll give you plenty to eat and drink and you can sleep in the little house outside, in the loft."

"And what about money?" I asked.

"Money!" says he. "I'll give you no money at all — but I'll give you something better if you're able to take it with you. As many sheep as you're able to throw over the gate below at the side of the road. What d'ye think of that?"

I thought it over. When I had done so I said it wasn't a bad bargain at all.

"I'm satisfied," I said. "It's a deal."

"It's a deal so," says the farmer.

And so it was. I can only tell the truth, they gave me the best of food and drink. Each mouthful was as sweet as honey, not a morsel of it I didn't relish. The farmer then showed me where I'd be sleeping. I went to sleep. And I slept as soundly as any white man ever.

I went to work the following morning with plenty of zeal. But I'm telling you when the day was over I was the weary man. Herding cows and running after sheep. Bringing armfuls of hay to the cattle and hauling buckets until I was ready to drop, the dog killing himself running everywhere for me. And of course that was nothing until I thought of my mother and the way she'd put her bones through her skin looking after me.

"Isn't it a pity I'm not at home," I said to myself.

I closed my eyes then. When I'd them opened again it was bright day and the farmer banging at the door. I truly believed there had been no night at all.

The day ahead was as bad as the day before. My legs and bones ached. And they weren't small pains either.

On the third day at dinner time the farmer's daughter brought me some food. Whatever way I was the two days previously I was in no shape at all now. I was banjaxed entirely. I was going to say that it was pointless going on, that I'd have to go home. But she was the first to speak.

"It would seem," says she, "that you have plenty to do."

"I have," says I, "and twice that much. I don't know will I be able to stand the work at all."

"Musha," says she laughing, "woe to whoever called you a good man. Do you want help?"

"Indeed and don't think of it," I said to her. "You needn't go dirtying your hands with my work."

But it was no good talking to her.

"I'm used to this work," says she.

While I was eating my dinner she had as much done as would take me the half day.

Many a time after that she gave me the helping hand and I didn't feel the work as heavy. Indeed, I didn't notice the time going by. I never felt the year and the day but it was up.

When it was, I went to the farmer looking for my wages. He was quite satisfied with me. Off we went down to the gate.

I thought of grabbing hold of a big fat ram that was there, thinking I'd get a fair penny for him at the market. But alas! I couldn't budge him from the ground, not to mention being able to throw him over the gate.

"That's fairly bad," says I to myself. "I'll take a sheep with me so." It was the same with the sheep.

Then I thought I'd take a few of the lambs with me and I wouldn't be doing too badly at all.

But easier said than done. I wasn't able to throw the smallest lamb over the gate.

The farmer was watching me and, of course, plenty satisfied with himself.

"I'm not able for any of them," I said.

"That's the way it is now," says he.

"Does that mean I won't be getting anything for my work?"

"That's the way it is now," says he.

"Damn your hide," says I.

But there was no point trying to get the better of him. He wouldn't part with a mite. He was as stingy as the devil.

"But I'll give you work," says he, "if you want it, for a year and a day."

"Keep your work," says I.

And I went off, cursing him to the sheep-white heavens. And so I walked empty handed until soon I had come to the same cross again. So it goes. "I'm as badly off now as I ever was," I said to myself. "I'm the same as I am."

* * *

"There you are again."

I turned around and who should I see but your man — the little grey fellow.

"It's yourself," says I, "bless you."

"My soul, it's myself," says he, "as you see me. How are you, you poor thing?"

"I'm in a hell of a predicament," says I and told him the story.

"Aha," says he "I knew that would happen. You're not the only one the farmer has tricked in this way. Come here," says he, "what kind of food did you get from him?"

"Oh, the best," says I, "the best of food."

"Did you get any meat from him?"

"My soul, I did," said I, which was true.

"Come here," says he, "did he give you any salt to shake on it?"

"Bedad, now that you mention it," says I, "that's something I didn't get. Not a grain of it."

"Indeed," says the little grey man, "it's no wonder you've no fizz in you. You shouldn't be surprised you couldn't throw the sheep over the gate."

I hadn't a clue what the poor man was trying to tell me. But I had an idea he was out for my good. I trusted him. There was something about him I liked.

"Maybe you're right," says I, "but what good is it talking about it now, what's the good of talk when the damage is done?" says I.

"Oh, that's not the way it is at all," says he, "if you follow my drift. Now is your chance — now that you know your way about, if you know what I mean."

Sure I might as well tell the truth — I still hadn't a clue what he was on about.

"What will I do so?" says I.

"Oh, sure, as simple as pie. Take a friend's advice and go back to that rapscallion of a farmer. Don't give him the satisfaction..."

"I'm not trying to be ahead of you," says I, "but wasn't I long enough with him and can't you see for yourself the doleful conclusion to all the work?"

"Don't worry a bit this time round," he said, "because I've something here that will assist you. See this bag?" says he, "it's full of salt. Take it with you. Put a wee grain of that on your dinner ever day... and, ahem, ahem... and you'd never know what would be the result. But on the skin of your ear, don't let the farmer see you and say nothing to nobody about it."

"I'll do that," says I, "and God keep you hearty."
I took the little bag. When I was about to say good luck to him he had vanished.

Gone into the mist.

"It's yourself," was the way the farmer greeted me when I crossed the door.

"More work you want is it?"

"Yes," says I.

We struck the same bargain. After a year and a day I'd have as my wages as many sheep as I was able to throw over the gate.

One would think a year and a day is a long time but I didn't notice it going by. Leoithne, the farmer's daughter, brought me dinner a lot of the time. She often helped me out when I had too much to do. But what I mostly noticed was that we were getting very friendly together. Very friendly indeed. But hadn't a poor person like me the nerve to be interested in the daughter of a well-heeled gent? I often told myself that. But if I did, it didn't stop me liking her. But we'll leave that, for a while.

A day didn't pass but I shook a small grain of salt on my dinner, unknown to all. And so it was.

Before long the year and the day were up and it was time for me to go and ask for my wages.

Like the previous year it was there ready for me. We went out into the field and down to the gate.

The farmer was in a mocking mood, the old devil.

"Here," says he and he sends a big ram over to me, "put your two arms around that one and throw him over the gate. Isn't it a pretty penny you'll get for him at the fair," and he killing himself with laughter. The ram came over to me. I put my two arms under his legs, lifted him up and threw him over the gate without a bother in the world.

I'm telling you the farmer was in no laughing mood now.

I caught hold of another one and performed the same feat. That was when the farmer came to me, pale of hue.

"Ha, for God's sake," says he, "leave me one or I'll be destroyed entirely..."

"It's little pity you had for me last year when you had the upper hand," says I. "Now you know my mettle."

"You're the finest man that ever I've seen," says he. "Never have I seen a man performing a deed you are able to do. But in God's name leave me my sheep."

"We have to comply with the bargain we made."

"We do, of course," says he, "but maybe we could come to some other arrangement now?"

"What would that be?" says I.

I had him on the run now.

We began bargaining and haggling and in the heel of the hunt he agreed I'd be master of half the farm. And wasn't that some upward mobility.

Myself changed greatly then. I hadn't a care in the world as we employed more servant boys. I was able to follow my own advice. But I wasn't completely satisfied yet. There were a few brambles yet on my path to clear.

Just because I was master of half the farm didn't mean I was leading the life of Reilley.

The farmer was a hard man to squeeze anything out of.

But I suppose he was none too pleased with me either. I had an inkling he was trying to get rid of me somehow. I'd be glad to be rid of him too, but I pretended nothing. I was hoping we'd come to some amicable agreement.

He came to me one day.

"Musha," says he, "maybe you'd be inclined to go off somewhere else on your own."

"I wouldn't mind," says I, which was true, because I'd often thought of the Glen and the way I could put a shape on it if only I had some money to spend on it.

"I was thinking" he said, "of buying half the farm back off you. I'd give you — oh, anything at all if you scadoodled."

We agreed then on a price that I thought fair enough. The two of us were as happy as the other. I considered it opportune to bring another matter up. It was the farmer himself that brought it up, though we hadn't the same mind about it; as I quickly found out.

"It's none of my business," says he, "but many the likes of you would be thinking of marrying at this time of your life."

"That's true," says I, "but it's easier to think of it than to do it."

"Oh, leave that to me," says he, but I didn't know was he having me on or was he serious.

"I know a young lass who would be very suited to you," he said. "A red head."

"Not for me," said I, "I wouldn't go for a red head."

"She'd be too good for you," says he. "I know one with black hair."

"Not for me, I wouldn't go for a black head."

'She'd be too good for you," says he. "I know a one that's blonde."

"Not for me I wouldn't go for a blonde."

"She'd be too good for you. But what will I do with you at all?" says he, "you can't be satisfied."

Who would be going by just then but his daughter and I suppose she overheard.

"There's the woman I'll have," says I.

When the farmer heard this he was speechless with anger. He roared. He bellowed. And I left him there and ran off with my money. I had to flee.

I came back later unbeknownst. But I didn't leave by myself this time because Leoithne was with me. And I'm not saying what happened then, because it's nobody's business what happens when a young woman elopes with her love to a pleasant Glen far away in Ireland long ago.

Spinning Maura

Spinning Maura lived a long while ago.

She was poor. Her man had died and she had a young family to raise. They had nothing but want.

On top of it all the landlord was threatening to take the spinning wheel if she hadn't the rent next time he called.

She had cause to be worried.

Herself and her family would be at their wit's end without the wheel, because that was all she had to earn enough to keep them alive. It wasn't easy for a poor widow to earn money.

But if God left her health to her, and the landlord the wheel, she'd be alright. That's what she said to herself, and to her family, many is the time.

"The wheel will see us through," she would say.

"The wheel will see us through now," she said referring to the present hardship. "I'll spin the wheel anyway."

She was in demand. The wheel sang. Maura didn't spare herself. She spun away; spinning and carding. People coming with wool and leaving with yarn. She spun from blackest night to blackest morning — yes, and sometimes too into the brightening day.

When her fame went out as a weaver people came from near and far asking her to weave some wool. Of course she wasn't working for nothing and before long she was piling the pennies on top of the other.

If she continued like that she would have the rent next time the landlord came. "Let him not thrive nor fatten on it, the scoundrel!"

The fine landlord didn't forget the appointed day for collection. Himself and his men and his horses were outside the house by first light. As usual, the milk of human kindness wasn't flowing from him. He wouldn't be long throwing some wretch out of house and home. God

17

pity the creature without the rent. Such was the law.

Ah, money's the fine lad. Many a time it's been said. If you have it in the pocket you can talk proudly to any man.

Spinning Maura had enough of the aforementioned to hand over to the lord on this pressing occasion.

She gave him the money and off he went — himself and his horses, and may the north wind go with them...

Maura had no worries now. Well, she had put one calamity aside anyway. But it wasn't plain sailing yet. They needed food. They needed clothes. Things that had to be paid for, even in those days. As Maura knew well.

She knew the meaning of want and she knew she didn't want it. She decided that this winter anyway they would have enough. Now that she had work to do, what harm to put a few pennies aside, for a rainy day.

She kept on weaving, all through the day and through the night.

She wasn't doing anything wrong, of course. Just working away nicely. It's no sin to work hard, or even too hard, as was the case with Maura. Nobody was forcing her. If she was worn out there was no one to blame but herself. It was nobody else's concern. She was harming no one. That's what she believed, the dear woman.

But there's another side to everything. She never thought her own story would have another side to it — but it did, and soon enough she'd know about it.

There was another crowd that didn't like these goings on at all: they were getting more and more annoyed as time went on.

Soon they'd lose their patience.

A quiet frosty night. Winter darkness. The mystery of Samhain letting itself be known. All was still. The quietness challenged by the creaking wheel. Spinning Maura was at it. Not noticing the dark quiet world around her.

Spinning Maura. The very dead of night.

19

She paused for a moment and threw a few sods on the fire. It was then she heard the rustling at the door. Or thought she heard. She listened carefully. Was there something at the door? Everything was quiet again. Ah, she was only dreaming. A sudden gust of wind teasing the torpor of the night.

It started again. It wasn't an ordinary wind either but a strange wispy fluttering the likes she hadn't heard in a long long time. From another domain. She took fright. She had an idea it meant no good.

It began again, a murmuring. Now she knew it was murmuring but for the life of her couldn't make out the talk that was going on.

The talk got more noisy. Ominous hub bub. Now she could understand some if it:

>Hoorla haarla
>Spinning Maura:
>Spin and weave
>Morn to eve!
>Hoorla haarla
>Spinning Maura:
>Morn to eve
>Spin and weave...

Over and over they keened and keened. Fading away, coming back again. Up and down and around.

Then something happened that Spinning Maura would never like to see the likes again. The door opened. It was the strange wind that opened it. And then they came in. It was them.

The good people.

But you wouldn't call them good now. They were horrendous. When Maura got her breath she stood there in amazement. No wonder. There was something about them that would put the fear of God in you. They had dark eyes and protruding teeth. A brazen looking lot.

The first one to come in sat himself on a stool by the north wall. He crossed his legs. Letting his head drop, all you could see of him was the big hat. And the two shoes.

Another one came in and sat beside him. A small rake of a man with a grand white cravat around his neck. He said nothing either.

So many of them had come in by now she couldn't make them all out. The kitchen teemed with them. Both sexes.

They had hurleys, sticks and sharp knives. They were on the warpath. None of them was very big, but none too small either. Some were thin and some were bloated. But they all had the same dark face on them.

The men wore grey coats and knee-breeches. The women coloured shawls and black dresses. She noticed they all had socks of bog cotton. But that's only part of it — she couldn't take in everything, so much was happening together. Coupled with that their strange voices had begun to weaken her brain.

They didn't speak directly to Maura at all. She thought, maybe, there was a taboo against that. That's not to say they weren't saying what they wanted to say, they were — in their own queer fashion.

As soon as they were in they started chanting in their own odd lingo. Implying all the time how outraged they were.

"D'ya see over there?" says one.

"D'ya see over there?" says another, in answer.

"An didn't we always hear —
Since we've been always there —
No matter how cheap or dear,
The night must get it's share..."

says one, giving the hearth a belt with his hurley and scattering ashes in the air.

"They'll leave us alone
With worries of our own,
And those that won't, I say.
Will pay, will pay, will pay..."

said a wisp of a little woman, dancing around, throwing razor shells in the air and catching them again with the greatest of ease. And another said:

21

"Give her the day,
The night is ours,
Put the wheel away,
For a couple of hours..."
And all together:
"Hoorla haarla
Spinning Maura..."
over and over. And then, with more force than ever before:
"Come here, come here,
Come here, come here:
The Pooka draws near
The Pooka draws near..."

Maura's heart froze. She believed she and her children, sleeping through all this, were in terrible danger. She didn't know what was best to do, but she knew something had to be done. She never saw the likes of these before, but she knew their ways were inclined to no good. Hopping around the house in ghoulish fashion. But the mention of the Pooka, that hadn't come yet, was what frightened her most.

"Musha musha," she cried pitifully, "how did I draw them down on me at all?"

She tried to talk to them and placate them but they took no notice of her. Maybe if she gave them something to eat, or to drink, it might do some good. She'd put down a fine pot of tea for them. Maybe when they had that inside them their anger might subside? Isn't many a time the little mug of tea melted her own peevishness? Sure wasn't it worth trying anyhow? But as ill-luck would have it, not a drop of water was left in the bucket. Of all the unfortunate times for it to happen. But the well wasn't too far away.

She rose up and grabbed the bucket. No one stopped her. I suppose they thought the night was long. They knew Maura wouldn't travel very far. The night was theirs. They were completely in control. They settled down nice and quietly. Waiting.

She went with the bucket to the well. Her mind was

upside down.

A fine moonlit night. She wasn't long going to the well and filling her bucket. The little well under the cliff was bubbling over.

Back she came in a hurry — not knowing under God's heaven what was best to do. In her haste she stumbled over a stone.

"Misfortune on you stone," she said angrily, "is it no where else you could have been?"

"Will you not be talkin' to me like that," said the stone.

Did the stone speak? Impossible. No one ever heard of stones talking before. But she heard more.

"Do you not recognise me?" said the stone.

Now she knew it was definitely the stone that was talking. God above! What a night!

"I'm afraid," says Maura, "I'm afraid I don't..."

"I'm your mother, dear. Listen carefully to what I have to say..."

"My mother, that's dead for years..."

"It's me surely — and don't be wasting time because every minute counts. Take heed of me now and you'll be better off. Listen now, carefully. That's a bad shower that's visiting you. There's two types of good people, those that are friendly and those that are not. Those that are not are in your house now and they won't be happy till they've had their revenge."

"But sure I did nothing on them," protested Maura.

"You didn't?" said the stone. "Upon my soul, that's not what I heard. What are you up to every night this long while now... yes, working at night, every single night. They don't like that one bit. The night is theirs. They keep a sharp eye on what's theirs and God look down on anyone that poaches on them, as you did..."

"But what'll I do now?"

"One thing you must do," the stone said. "This is what you must do: when you go home now, stay outside the door and let you start howling. At the very top of your voice say Cnoc Meá is on fire. You'll see yourself then what will happen."

"And is Cnoc Meá in flames?"

"It is no such thing — but don't mind that you, just say it."

She was going to race off — and then she got curious. It's not often she'd get the chance to find out what goes on in the other world. She'd put a few questions now.

"Tell me," says she to the stone.

"Tell me nothing," says the stone, "and off you go in a hurry and if you fall don't pause to get up..."

That was the end of the talking and the stone was as quiet and as mute as any other stone on the side of the road.

Maura took off in a hurry.

She became afraid as she approached the house. They were still there. Sitting quietly around the kitchen. Waiting.

When Maura came near the flagstone by the front door she threw the bucket aside and started to howl:

"Cnoc Meá is on fire.

"Cnoc Meá is on fire."

When the crowd inside heard this they got up in a hurry and absconded one on top of the other. They took off like the wind.

Maura was as quick as them going in. When she found herself inside, she bolted the door. Wasn't it she that was grateful the trick worked.

She sent her blessing to the stone, if stone it was, that had given her the advice.

She wouldn't touch the wheel again that night, or any other night either. She was still frightened a bit. She couldn't forget the night's adventures. She waited. She listened. She heard nothing. Nothing was disturbing the stillness now. Everything was nice and peaceful. She tasted the calm that comes with the night.

The Hand

I was always slightly ill at ease — even from the day I was born, to tell the truth. There was nothing really very wrong with me and you'd want to be sharp-eyed to notice anything amiss in the first place. But my father and mother knew.

It was my left hand, God save us. I never budged it.

A little child usually stretches out his two hands eagerly, as though trying to grasp the unknown. His desire for life, contrary as it is.

But I wasn't that way at all. I'd stretch out my right hand like most people, nearly. But as to the left it would lie dead beside me.

You might think it no great inconvenience to have a lifeless left hand. But in my case it was the worst possible thing, because I was left handed. If it were my right hand that was useless, things wouldn't have been half so bad. But sorrows come, not in single spies, but in left-handed battalions! Naturally my father and mother were greatly put out.

"Thanks be to God there's nothing else wrong with him at any rate," says my mother. "He looks fine apart from the handeen."

"You can be sure there's nothing else wrong with him, see how closely he observes everything," said my father, his voice coloured with pride and sorrow.

I was lying down without a twitch out of me. As soon as I heard that talk, and they'd talk like that often, I stirred and let out a roar. I scowled terribly as if to say go off and gawk at someone else.

Of course I don't remember that particular occasion. How would I? I was five or six years in the world before I took an interest in anything. I was as happy with my left hand as I was with anything else. I had no idea then that my left wasn't quite right, so to speak.

25

My mother thought differently. So did the doctors and the nurses who came to wonder at me. A curse on them. "Take hold of that... no, with the other hand," they'd say, and me doing everything except what they wanted me to do.

But apart from such small matters my life was happy enough. Because of my hand I didn't have to do any work. Nobody expected help from me. What work could I do with my lifeless limb?

Something I had no time at all for and that was school. Wouldn't put a foot in the door if I had my way. I boasted I'd never go to school at all. But the day came and I had to go. Not without strong protest I assure you.

"You can cry the last tear remaining in your head," said my father sternly, "go you must. It's bad enough me being an ignoramus without you following me."

I didn't spend too long going to school though, a few years. I managed to learn a couple of things my own way. I was fairly good at reading but not great at writing.

I was so pleased to be allowed to stay away from school altogether. That was around the time, funny enough, that I became interested in learning. I began rummaging in the box of books Grandfather left behind when he died. Instead of being outside playing with the other children, I'd be going through the books, looking at them, wiping away the dust of years.

I read them very poorly at first but gradually made some sense of them. Nobody else was interested in them.

Grandfather's specs were in the box too. Sometimes I'd put them on for fun. When people would see me they'd be in stitches.

"Isn't it a strange thing," they'd say, "how like his Grandfather he is."

"And if he is what harm," my mother would say. "Grandfather was fine but for his angry spasms. Nothing wrong with the swipe of *his* left hand."

I'd give the table an awful crack with the stick then and let a yelp out of me the way Grandfather would when

26

roused. This would cause more laughter. That's how I spent my time.

I hardly noticed the years going by. I was in my teens before I knew it. By which time I was well used to the world and my disability.

Everbody was kind to me. But even if they were I had figured that they hadn't quite the same *meas* on me that they would if my left hand was what it should be.

There was never any chance of getting any real work to do. Without two hands I couldn't go rowing in a curragh. And there were lots of other tasks too for which I was unfit. But those were things I didn't want to do anyway. That's what I told myself at any rate. What can't be cured must be endured.

There were neighbours of ours who had it in for my father. They were Cartys. I didn't know then and I don't know now what caused the spite, if there was any reason for it at all. I might as well be truthful about it and say my father had it in for them as well.

Many was the bone of contention between them but nothing caused more furore than the fencing walls. I could never understand, nor was it ever explained to me, how fencing walls could cause such animosity.

But one thing I knew. I didn't like the falling out, one bit. I never thought that I'd be dragged into it before long — against my will, needless to say.

I was out bringing the tea to my father. That was the custom. A bottle of tea stuck in a stocking, some pieces of bread wrapped in a cloth, and these shoved into a small bag I would bring to the gang at work.

My father drank the tea contentedly. He left me a sup and a piece of bread. That was his habit, poor man. He went working then.

I sat beside the fencing wall drinking my mouthful of tea, looking at my father at work. He was clearing an area of stony ground that was flecked with little patches of grass. He was building a wall too.

It was a great strain to lift those stones and carry them to the wall. I longed with all my heart to be able to help him. But I didn't want to go near him in case I'd rouse him to tell me get out of the way, saying: "Where would you be going with your one hand," or some such phrase that I didn't want to imagine.

You'd think he was able to read my mind because he looked across at me.

"Be off home you," he said. "You might have to go to the shop, or something... good man. Take the dog with you." He knew I'd like that.

I started to put things into the bag. I saw my father looking at a large slab.

"An awful pity to break it," he said.

He tried to turn it over. He put such a strain on himself my greatest fear was he'd have a heart attack with all the effort. He let it down again.

"Ah, I'll have to break it."

I said nothing aloud but in my own mind I was saying: if you'd listened to me you'd have broken it long ago. But it wasn't my business. I was supposed to be going home.

I was just going out the gap when I heard a commotion coming down the boreen. And a commotion it was to be sure. My father's enemy, Carty, and his son, who was about my own age, approaching like a black storm.

"Interfering with your neighbour's property?" was the threatening greeting from Carty. Carty went to the wall, moved some stones and began to throw down a few.

"Bad luck to you," my father said, or some such phrase, "don't knock the wall."

"Who'll stop me?"

"My soul, you might be stopped easily enough."

My father looked at me and I knew what was in his mind: 'I'm on my own rightly.' I was afraid someone might get killed because you'd never know what moment but they might start throwing stones at one another. They were shouting at each other by now and you wouldn't know what they were saying.

Whenever a *rí-rá* like this broke out I'd normally say nothing. Who'd take any notice of me? I'd keep away from fights. But now I was caught in the middle.

Maybe it was time I had a change of attitude. Hadn't I the gift of speech like anybody else? I had to do something...

I threw away the bag. Fear left me and I felt something else in its place. Courage. A desire to act. Over I go. Carty's son started laughing at me and the shape I was throwing.

"What's all this shouting?" I said slowly, a challenge in my voice.

"The devil take me," said Carty, "Would you look at the grasshopper that's after arriving!"

I picked up an old stick that was lying on the ground and up I went, up on a big granite stone beside me. I cracked the stick on the stone the way I'd do when imitating Grandfather.

"A ha!" I said the way Grandfather would, swinging the stick.

"Ye're making a lot of noise there like a herd of goats and there's neither rhyme nor reason to any of it. But ye'll listen to me now."

Carty's son began to throw pebbles at me, teasing me, but Carty himself told him to stop, "for a while, at any rate."

I made one hell of a great speech then — though I say so myself.

I spoke of the strong hand and the weak. I told them of things that I had thought about all the times away on my own, or sitting in the chimney-corner reading the books. What I stressed most of all was the way people are always fighting with each other and tormenting each other — and how easy it was to settle things, if there was a will.

"That's the way it is with you," I said.

They were listening. I think they lost their tongues with wonderment — as they watched and listened.

I still didn't know what they thought of my tirade. As

I had started I might as well finish.

"The long and the short of it is," said I, "that we have a chance now to make up — that or to be fighting about it for all time."

"Musha," says Carty, recovering from the shock he'd got, "you have a power of talk anyway whatever class of fairy you are... but be advised that it's not that easy to hoodwink me."

"We're not trying to hoodwink you at all, as well you know. We're only trying to come to terms..."

"Ye lot, coming to terms! It's well I know what that means, as always ye'll want the cream..."

"Tell me so," says I coming back at him, "where do you think the boundary should be...?"

"Not where ye're building the wall and that's for sure," he said walking away from us. He came to a stone that was jutting out of a cleft.

"There's the boundary stone," he said. "And there's another," pointing to a stone some distance away. "There's another one."

"If that's the way you want to have your wall," said my father, "it will be an interesting one. It will be as crooked as a dog's hind leg."

"That is how the old ones long ago settled the boundaries."

"It certainly is not," said my father. "I'm every bit as old as yourself and never heard of such a boundary."

"There's lots of things you've never heard," came the snappy reply from Carty. "You didn't want to hear it — and that's what it is."

I thought it was time to intervene once more in case they'd get to bettering each other once again.

"Can't we draw the boundary straight and divide equally among us?" I said.

"That will be the day," says Carty, "when ye'll divide equally..."

"You divide it so," I said boldly. "We'll leave it to you."

31

Carty was taken aback a while, but talk came to him soon enough.

"Indeed I'll have nothing to do with you or your wall... That's it now. You have no permission to build the wall."

"We can build on half it, can't we?"

"I suppose..."

"No 'suppose' about it but sure and certain," said my father. "We'll build half the wall."

"I suppose," says Carty walking east towards the stony area, his son behind him.

"Ye're a hard lot to please," said my father giving them a surly look. And then he looked to the heavens, imploringly, as though asking on God to resolve the whole thing.

The Cartys were gone by now. I was about to make tracks. I had the bag on my shoulder. My father noticed me.

"It's not going you are?" he said.

I said nothing.

"Leave me alone," he said, "with no one to speak up for me or say what's right?"

"Me?"

"Who else?" he said, "sure there's none to beat you. You stumped Carty today and that was no mean feat." He was serious.

I didn't know what to say. I wasn't used to praise. Somehow I felt my status had changed.

When my father told me to saddle the horse and bring her home I was delighted — but not a bit surprised.

Night Ructions

It was night, almost. The boy was in a hurry. Didn't fancy being caught in the dark. But it wouldn't be all that black, he thought. Hadn't he been playing on the road the night before and all was bright as the living day.

Never mind that. He wouldn't like to be going down Barr N'ána too late as it was an eerie spot.

"Sure, I'll throw in a couple of stones," he said as he built up the gap. They'd never go over the two stones."

He meant the small flock of sheep and the big ram that were gathered in the middle of the mound and appeared to be happy enough with themselves. And why wouldn't they be?

They had plenty of grass. They wouldn't be there at all, of course, were it not so late and the boy not able to bring them out any further on the crags.

He threw a few stones in the gap as planned and hurried off.

The sheep stood immobile in the middle of the ground at first but bit by bit they began to graze.

Night spread over the island. The sky darkened at first but then began to grey, and night took on its own shape.

The moon or a sliver of moon was somewhere but was hidden by a frosty vapour that filled the entire sky. You couldn't say it was dark. Maybe, even, the moon was full somewhere, busily penetrating the film of hoar.

The spirit of night was activating all things around. Reminding the bird it was time to doze. It drove the boy home. Night's business is best left to the night.

The same spirit had got into the big ram. In this charged atmosphere he glimpsed the reason and the importance of his being. An inexplicable feeling coursed through his blood. He could feel an inborn strength beginning to manifest itself and sensed the dignity and power which is the stamp of sovereignty.

And who could dispute his rule? Not alone on this mound. Anywhere! Still, he kept himself in check.

Shaking himself vigorously he went off in search of some sweet grass.

The moon was somewhere.

By this time it was fully night. The peace which most earth creatures desire was palpable in the air.

But also coming to a head was that giddiness which night inspires in its more adventurous denizens.

The big ram was one of that minority which night calls to high-headed deeds.

Like all his kind, he got little opportunity to prove himself, confined as he was to his own domain.

But things would change tonight!

He looked at the few stones casually thrown in the gap by the boy — the only obstacle between him and the wide world. He could see how easily he might toss them aside.

This was the chance he had been waiting for.

Whenever this night-time fitfulness got hold of him nothing could satisfy him but to break loose.

Hemmed in feeling... What wouldn't he give to be out there and show the strutting high and mighty who was in charge.

Suddenly the stones were down.

Baa-a-a. The sheep startled and huddled together in the centre of the mound, seeing it was the big ram that had caused the furore.

They knew the big fellow was out for ructions. Nothing would stop him now.

On the road. Free. He could do anything he liked now, as nature prodded him.

The sheep followed. One after the other. Following him out on the road. Not knowing where they were going. He didn't quite know himself. But he was on his way.

He went out past the Old Milking Place. Stopped at Beartleen's Gap — nothing much there to rouse him. Out again.

It was still and you could hear his keen footfall coming

through the eerie wisps of night. The sheep straggling behind.

Cló Naomh. Nothing stirring here. The procession continued.

They stopped at *Róidín na bPúcaí.* Momentarily between two minds. Down the boreen or stay on the road? Stay on the road. On. And on.

They passed *Crogán a' Cheannaigh. Creig na gCruibíní. Róidín an Phríosúin. Buailtín 'n tSagairt.* Towards *Macha — Macha Mór.* On to *Ceann an Bhóthair.*

There was more. Though the road stopped suddenly a great expanse lay beyond. Where the ditch crossing the road ended were two gaps. One to the right, the other to the left. A ditch separating the two gaps, dividing two mounds.

The big ram made for the east gap. The mound to the east.

It had sheep. Scattered here and there along the mound. Some lying down.

In among them the Young Ram. Proud as a king. He heard the commotion at the gap. A fit of pique. He recognised the Big Ram.

And the Big Ram recognised him. And he knew that it was this young ram that had made him frantic all night. He felt his blood seething, goading him on. He would face fiercely any foe that dared countenance him.

That challenge awaited him beyond the gap. Now that he was free and unfettered it would be so easy just to walk in.

The fellow inside was in fighting fettle too. He also wanted to assert his supremacy. He wanted to be free and display to the world what prowess he could command.

They faced one another. The Big Ram and the Young Ram. They didn't spend long sizing each other up. There was no holding them now. They were free to lash into the fray.

Crash! Two skulls collided. All a-tremble. The

Young Ram more badly shaken. Lost his ground. The big fellow's next assault threw him even futher back. It was clear that the Big Ram had more fire and wind.

The Young Ram backed off. Fell. Up again in a flash. Faced the Big Ram, again and again. Collapsing, again and again...

They moved to the outer edge of the mound. Through hollow and hillock. Over soft ground and stone. The Young Ram falling, retreating...

Until they came to the ditch outside. *The wall of Macha.* The Young Ram had no where else to go. But he wouldn't yield. He faced the Big Ram...

And the Big Ram faced him — standing on his two hind legs and pumping all his strength into every shape he made.

The Young Ram didn't know where he was, or in what world... The next onrush floored him completely.

All feet in the air. Tongue out. He had it. For good.

The Big Ram had done the deed. He turned back. But, trying to walk, the legs buckled under him. On his knees. Attempting to rise he crashed over on his side.

A little glen behind him. He rolled down on his side. Couldn't get up.

For a while his legs were twisting and turning like a dog having a dream. Then the legs stiffened and the Big Ram lay motionless — not a twitch.

The sky had brightened. The frost of earlier was on the run and the moonlight streamed through.

Nightclouds moved silently, peacefully. The sky smiled. The Goddess of the night smiled...

Satisfied, it would seem.

Fuadar Oíche

Bhí sé ina oíche, beagnach. Bhí deifir ar an mbuachaill. Níor mhaith leis go mbéarfadh an oíche air. Ach ní oíche dhorcha a bheadh inti, cheap sé. Nach raibh sé ag imirt ar an mbóthar an oíche roimhe sin agus nach raibh sí chomh geal leis an lá.

Ach ba chuma sin. Níor mhaith leis a bheith ag dul síos Barr N'ána ródhéanach mar is áit uaigneach a bhí ann.

"Ara, caithfidh mé cúpla cloch inti," a dúirt sé leis féin, agus é ag tógáil na bearna.

"Ar ndóigh, ní ghabhfadh siad sin thar dhá chloch."

Bhí sé ag tagairt don scata beag caorach agus don reithe mór a bhí bailithe le chéile i lár an chreagáin agus an chuma orthu go raibh siad sásta go maith leo féin. Agus cén fáth nach mbeadh?

Bhí neart féir ansin acu. Ar ndóigh, ní bheidís ann ar chor ar bith murach an deireanas agus dá bharr nach bhféadfadh an buachaill iad a thabhairt amach níos faide ar na creaga.

Chaith an buachaill an cúpla cloch sa mbearna mar a bhí beartaithe aige — agus d'imigh leis faoi dheifir.

D'fhan na caoirigh ina meall i lár an chreagáin ar dtús ach de réir a chéile thosaigh siad ag iníor.

Leath an oíche í féin ar fud an oileáin. Dhorchaigh an spéir ar dtús agus ansin thosaigh sí ag liathú nó go raibh dreach sainiúil na hoíche uirthi.

Bhí an ghealach, nó píosa di, in áit éigin ach bhí sí múchta ag an gcuisne a bhí spréite gach ceárd den spéir. Ach ní fhéadfaí a rá go raibh sí dorcha. B'fhéidir, fiú amháin, go raibh an ghealach lán uile agus go raibh sí i bhfolach in áit éigin agus ag síothlú tríd an gcuisne liath.

Bhí spiorad na hoíche ag dul i bhfeidhm ar an nádúr máguaird. Mheabhraigh sé don éan go raibh sé in am suain. Díbir sé an buachaill abhaile. Fágtar cúraimí na hoíche faoin oíche.

Agus bhí an spiorad céanna ag dul i bhfeidhm ar an

38

Agus bhí an spiorad céanna ag dul i bhfeidhm ar an reithe mór. San atmaisféar mistéireach seo thuig sé an gá agus an tábhacht a bhí leis féin. Bhraith sé mothú domhínithe ag bíogadh ina chuid fola.

D'airigh sé an neart a bhí ann ó nádúr á chur féin in iúl. Bhraith sé ann féin an mhórgacht agus an chumhacht is dual don té a bhíonn ina rí agus i gceannas.

Agus ar ndóigh, nárbh é an ceannasaí é. Agus ní ar an gcreagán seo amháin é, ach ar chuile chreagán eile. Ach choinnigh sé guaim air féin.

Chroith sé é féin go bríomhar agus d'imigh leis siar an creagán ag soláthar greim blasta féir.

Bhí an ghealach in áit éigin.

Bhí an oíche ina hoíche amach is amach faoi seo. Bhí an suaimhneas a shantaíonn formhór mhuintir an tsaoil le linn na hoíche le mothú go forleathan.

Ach bhí an eachtraíocht a spreagann an oíche in aicme ghuaisbheartach amháin de mhuintir an tsaoil ag teacht in uachtar go tréan freisin.

Bhí an reithe mór i measc an mhionlaigh sin a mbíonn fonn gnímh agus éirí in airde orthu san oíche. Ach, dála an dreama sin uile, ní mórán cead gnímh a d'fhaigheadh an reithe mór — mar bhíodh sé cuibhrithe laistigh dá ghiodán féin.

Ach bheadh athrú ar an scéal sin anocht!

D'fhéach sé ar an gcúpla cloch a bhí caite go fánach ag an mbuachaill roimhe sa mbearna — an t-aon bhac a bhí idir é agus an saol mór. D'aithin sé cé chomh héasca is a bhí sé dó iad a chaitheamh anuas.

Seo í an fhaill a raibh sé ag tnúth léi.

Nuair a bhuaileadh an spadhar oíche seo é ní bhíodh sé sásta ná leathshásta nuair nach mbíodh cead amach aige. Bhraitheadh sé brúite faoi chois... B'fhearr leis ná rud maith a bheith amuigh le go gcruthódh sé do lucht an éirí in airde is an ghaisce cérbh é an máistir.

Go tobann thit na clocha...

Baa-a-a. Phreab na caoirigh agus chruinnigh siad le

chéile i lár an chreagáin. Thug siad faoi deara gurb é an reithe mór a bhí ag réabadh.

Thuig siad go raibh fonn gleo ar an bhfear mór. Ní stopfadh dada anois é.

Anois bhí sé ar an mbóthar. Bhí sé saor. Bhí deis aige anois rud ar bith ba mhian leis a dhéanamh de réir mar a threoródh a nádúr é.

Agus lean na caoirigh é. Ceann i ndiaidh a chéile. Lean siad amach an bóthar é. Ach ní raibh a fhios acu cá raibh siad ag dul. Ní raibh a fhios aige féin ceart go fóill é. Ach bhí sé ar a bhealach.

Chuaigh sé amach thar an tsean-bhuaile. Stop sé ag Bearna Bheairtlín — ach ní raibh dada ansin a thug a dhúshlán. Amach leis.

Bhí an oíche ciúin agus chloisfeá torann díocasach a chos ag teacht trí néalta diamhair na hoíche. Bhí na caoirigh ag teacht ina dhiaidh go fánach agus go neamhrialta.

Cló Naomh. Ní raibh dúshlán ar bith ansin. Lean an mórshiúl orthu.

Stop siad ag Róidín na bPúcaí. Idir dhá chomhairle ar feadh nóiméid. An ngabhfadh sé soir an róidín nó an bhfanfadh sé ar an mbóthar? Amach. Amach.

Ghlan siad amach Crogán a' Cheannaigh. Greig na gCrúibíní. Róidín an Phríosúin. Buailtín 'na tSagairt. I dtreo Mhacha — an Macha Mór. I dtreo Cheann an Bhóthair.

Níorbh é Ceann an Bhóthair an deireadh. Cé gur stop an bóthar go tobann bhí fairsinge mhór eile amach uaidh. An claí a bhí ag trasnú an bhóthair á chríochnú bhí dhá bhearna ann. Ceann taobh thoir agus ceann taobh thiar. Bhí claí idir an dá bhearna ag dealú dhá chreagán óna chéile laistigh.

Go dtí an bhearna thoir a chuaigh an reithe mór. An creagán thoir. Ar an gcreagán seo bhí scata caorach. Iad scaipthe anonn is anall. Cuid acu ina luí.

Ina measc bhí an Reithe Óg. É chomh mórálach le rí. D'airigh sé an trup-trap ag an mbearna. Chuir sé anmhúisiam air. D'aithin sé an Reithe Mór.

Agus d'aithin an Reithe Mór é. D'aithin sé chomh maith gurbh é an reithe óg seo ba shiocair leis an bhfuadar buile seo a bhí faoi anocht. D'airigh sé a chuid fola ag coipeadh á ghríosadh. Thabharfadh sé aghaidh go danartha ar namhaid ar bith a mbeadh sé de dhánaíocht ann a dhúshlán a thabhairt.

Bhí an dúshlán sin ag fanacht leis taobh istigh den bhearna. Ós rud é go raibh sé saor is gan cheangal bhí sé éasca go maith dó a dhul isteach go dtí é...

Bhí fonn troda ar an bhfear istigh freisin. Theastaigh uaidh féin a mháistreacht a thaispeáint. Theastaigh uaidh a bheith saor agus a thaispeáint chomh bithbhuach dochloíte a bhí sé. Chuir sé gothaí troda air féin...

Bhí an dá reithe ar aghaidh a chéile faoi seo. An Reithe Mór agus an Reithe Óg.

Níor fhan siad i bhfad ag breathnú ar a chéile. Ní raibh ceangal ná bac anois orthu. Bhí siad saor chun an ruathar éachtach seo a thabhairt...

Plimp! Bhuail an dá bhaithis in aghaidh a chéile. Croitheadh an péire. Ach croitheadh an Reithe Óg ní ba mhó. Cuireadh in aghaidh a thóna é.

Chuir an chéad phléisc eile ón bhfear mór ar a chúl tuilleadh é. B'fhurasta aithint go raibh spreacadh agus teacht aniar níos mó sa Reithe Mór.

Chúlaigh an Reithe Óg roimhe. Thit sé. Ach d'éirigh sé arís láithreach. Thug aghaidh arís agus arís eile ar an Reithe Mór. Arís agus arís eile thit sé...

Ghluais siad amach i dtreo cheann amuigh an chreagáin. Iad ag dul thar ísleáin agus ardáin. Thar bhogán agus thar chruachán. An Reithe Óg ag titim agus ag cúlú...

Nó gur bhuail siad an claí amuigh. Claí Mhacha. Go dtí nach bhféadfadh an Reithe Óg cúlú ní ba mhó. Ach níor ghéill sé. Thug sé aghaidh ar an Reithe Mór...

Agus thug an Reithe Mór aghaidh air — ag éirí ar a dhá chois deiridh agus ag cur iomlán a nirt le chuile iarraidh dar tharraing sé...

41

Anois ní raibh a fhios ag an Reithe Óg cá raibh sé, ná cén saol a raibh sé air..

Fogha amháin eile agus bhí sé sínte. A cheithre chos in aer. A theanga amuigh. Bhí a chuid aige. Ní dhúiseodh sé arís choíche.

Bhí an t-éacht déanta ag an Reithe Mór. Chas sé thar n-ais. Ach nuair a shíl sé siúl is é an chaoi ar lúb a dhá chos tosaigh faoi. Cuireadh ar a ghlúine é. Rinne sé iarracht éirí ach is amhladih a cuireadh anuas ar a thaobh é.

Bhí gleann beag taobh thiar de agus d'iompaigh sé siar ann ar a thaobh. Chinn sé air éirí.

Ar feadh tamaill bhí a chosa ag lúbadh is ag casadh cosúil le gadhar a bheadh ag brionglóideach. Sula i bhfad shín na cosa agus d'fhan an Reithe Mór ina staic — gan cor as.

Bhí an spéir níos gile faoi seo. An cuisne a bhí ann i dtús na hoíche bhí sé ag glanadh anois agus solas na gealaí ag teacht tríd.

Bhí néalta na hoíche ag gluaiseacht leo go mall síochánta anois. Bhí aoibh ar an spéir. Bhí aoibh ar Bhandia na hoíche...

Is cosúil go raibh sí sásta.

The Toy

Pookahs are plentiful around Hallowe'en. I'm not talking about those people that dress up, but real pookahs. The odd person has seen them. Maybe many people. Many have heard them moving about.

Of course there's a lot of people who have never seen them, who have never even heard them, and still and all they're terribly wary of them. And it's not around Samhain that they're scared of them either.

It's said that some of the pookahs are friendly and others not so. I myself am of the opinion that it's the ones from strange parts that are by far the worst because you wouldn't know what they'd be talking about...

My aunt sent me an unusual present from America. It was a curious little figureen that she had chosen for me as a toy. Although not outlandish in any way, you'd think, nevertheless it seemed somewhat out of place or somehow not able to adapt to our island envirnonment.

I don't think it would have been out of the ordinary back in the States. It would appear that such things are quite common in that country, as mantlepiece ornaments or for the purposes of puppeteering...

When the parcel arrived with my own name on it I was overjoyed. You never saw such joy. It was always a great occasion for me to get a new toy which I suppose proves (if proof be needed) that I was no different from other kids my age. The little figureen was made of plaster. It wore a longish green coat and a southwester type hat. Its cheeks were red. Another queer thing about it, two big boots.

He did nothing. But his two hands were always deep in his pockets. Always. He stood six inches tall. And that's all I can say about the way he looked, poor man.

A piece of cord through the loop on the top of the hat made it possible for us to hang him up anywhere that

43

suited. That's the life he had for a long while — hanging from the loft beam looking down on us all. He didn't bother a soul and nobody took any notice of him, except myself. After all, he was mine.

When there was no one else about I'd talk to him. I used to have great fun. Sometimes I'd stand on the big stool which brought me up to his level. I'd be peering into his beady black eyes.

He wasn't a great one for talking himself. Not that I expected him to say anything. But my father, if he can be believed, said he heard him come out with something. A morning he got up early to go fishing he heard him. Irish it wasn't and it wasn't English either.

It was Latin, the father said. I don't know how he made out it was Latin but I suppose he thought it sounded like the Mass.

But nobody else heard a syllable from him in any tongue. The father was having us on, we'd say and gradually we forgot all about it.

Nobody was surprised when I nicknamed him *Ciúineadas,* the Quiet One. They all agreed my choice of name was appropriate.

But it's little they knew, no more than myself at the time, that the name didn't suit him that well after all. If only they knew what I found out later on!

It was only through chance that I made this particular discovery.

It was pookah time, around Hallowe'en, but maybe that has nothing at all to do with the story. My mother was gone somewhere — to the shop, maybe, or Mass or somewhere... out to the garden to get cabbage perhaps... I wasn't a bit worried about her. I knew well she wouldn't leave the island. I wasn't at all lonely.

I was sitting in the middle of the floor, playing with saucepans. I soon started thinking about my silent friend. I got the big stool from the north wall and dragged it under the loft. Up I go.

I began to talk to him, as was usual for me, and playing with him. I felt sorry for him and regretted not having Latin so that I could talk to him in his own language. But even if I had the Latin how did I know he'd talk to me. It's unlikely he had any talk in him.

I should find out if he has or not, I said to myself, trying to think of a way to get him to talk.

"I'll get talk out of you yet if it kills me," I said jumping off the stool. Sense won't come before age, they say, and that was true in my case. Five years old I was and terribly lacking in sense.

And do you know what evil deed came into my head? Wait until I tell you.

I go the tongs. The next thing you know I had a blazing sod from the heart of the fire. The next thing you know I was up on the stool and placed the sod on the nose of my quiet little friend who never harmed a soul. God save us... He let out the most lamentable screech and as I jumped down from the stool I thought I saw tears coming from his black beady eyes. That was when I knew I had done a terrible deed.

He didn't say a word. What determination!

Yes, I knew I had done a foul deed and trembled. But what could I do?

What's done is done. I was only five and sense doesn't come that early. But that was poor consolation for *Ciúineadas,* himself and his burnt black nose. But he said nothing. No swear word, nor did he curse me or threaten revenge. He stayed quiet.

I was greatly upset by what had happened, but I wasn't going to tell a soul. They wouldn't believe me anyway. Whatever I'd say it would only be nonsense. They'd only laugh out loud if I told them. As it happened I didn't have to tell them because nobody was interested. They had other things on their minds. Wasn't Hallowe'en coming, there'd be sport and frolics — everyone's heart was brimming in anticipation.

Except mine. Not a day went by that didn't increase

my worry. I didn't know good from bad. I never thought of playing with him anymore. He made me ill at ease. For all I knew he could have been plotting revenge, the old devil.

From then on I'd never stay in the house alone, if you promised me the wide world. But I acted as if nothing had happened.

I often thought of going up to him and asking his pardon. Easier said than done: he had no Irish, the devil. Anyway I didn't think it would do much good to say I was sorry. The harm was done and all I could do was wait for him — wait for him to strike. What a terrible mess. And he waiting for the right moment...

And I didn't have to wait long...

Hallowe'en was over. All of us were passing the winter at our ease, or trying to anyway.

One night supper was over and we were preparing to sit around the fire, whiling away the rest of the night. I was showing my appreciation by helping with the washing up and putting the dishes away.

As I innocently crossed the room to put something on the dresser I noticed a thing that fairly rattled me. What was it but himself about to take a dive down on me, aflame with black mischief.

Without even thinking I leaped out of the way when I saw the calamity coming. I wasn't safe yet. He came after me. I went berserk around the house, shouting and leaping like a loon.

He pursued me, in leaps and bounds, but never uttering a sound. Hopping along on his belly he was.

I'll be grateful to my father until my dying day for it was he that saved me on that fateful night. He grabbed the little man and held him.

"Do you see," he said, "how the cord got stuck to your shoe." He was quite annoyed at this stage. Taking hold of the cord he lifted the figureen and threw him as far as he could out on the crags. The fright I'd got had put him in a thorny mood.

"What sort of ructions were you up to," he says to me, "sure you didn't think the toy was going to take a bite out of you, did you?"

"I don't know," I said and everybody started to laugh. But it was true, I didn't know.

"It's a pity they can't keep their dainties over yonder where they belong," said my mother and that put an end to it.

We never since heard whisper or tidings of the upstart of a figureen that was once my silent friend.

Out on my Own

I had only the dog with me. He was in more of a hurry than I was. Dogs are always in a hurry. Chasing something, I suppose — but I wouldn't know really.

But I knew right well why I was in a hurry. I'd been let out.

Grandfather. It was he had given me the road. It was he who had opened the door and said good luck. Nobody gave the dog permission to go. He didn't need it. He took a leap over the half door and shot up the road, as airy as a kid goat. Delighted to be out — like myself.

As for Grandfather. I can't make him out at all. It's hard to figure him. Sometimes he talks to himself. Sometimes directly to me. Other times I can't make out is it to myself or himself he's talking. But I like him. He doesn't quarrel with me or shoot off his mouth much with me. Even if he did I wouldn't be a bit afraid of him...

My mother gave him strict warning not to let the "little man" — that's me — outside.

"And also, mind you don't let him near the fire — because he's most unfortunate when he gets up to things he shouldn't be..."

"Oh, I'll keep him away from the fire," said poor Grandfather, "have no fear. I'll keep him from the sparks, I'm telling you. I'll take this stick to his arse," says he, putting on a fierce expression.

My mother went off then, leaving Grandfather in the chimney corner smoking his pipe and me poking around in corners, whiling away the time... and the dog lying in a sunbeam.

We were like that for a while. Nothing wondrous happened at all. But then suddenly, Grandfather spoke:

"Will you be tending any cow at all today?" says he, looking at me surlily.

I took no notice at all of him. Sure I thought it was

49

yapping away to himself he was. But it wasn't long before he started expostulating again!

"Come here to me," says he, "what kind of a class of a fellow are you at all that you won't go to the cow — and the day flying past..."

I tried to explain to him that he shouldn't be going on about cattle to me, that he should be talking to himself, but he wouldn't listen.

"Come come come," says he, ordering me about, "get your can and out you go, step on it, or have you no shame to be off milking at this hour of the day? Off with you!"

Up he goes to the door and gazes out.

"Oh, musha, what a grand day it is," says he, "and nothing done yet in the house..."

He opened the half-door...

"Out you go boy and put a shape on yourself. Come on now..."

I was out. Free to wander. It wasn't long before I was taking great strides up the little road, the keen spirit of spring urging me onwards. Wasn't fortune smiling on me.

And where would a five year old adventurer like myself be off to this fine spring morning?

There was many a spot I could turn to. But at this stage I couldn't care less. I was out, and that was enough for the moment.

I'd follow my nose, as Grandfather would say. God keep you, Grandfather.

And my nose didn't bring me very far. I went east another little road, a windy stony boreen full of brambles. The odd nettle too, surveying my bare feet and ready for me with a sting. But that wouldn't stop me.

My dog ahead of me. Lively and neat.

The boreen took a turn. In the corner, a most curious thing. The townland well. I couldn't go on without spending a while there. I'd heard of it from Grandfather and others.

But I heeded Grandfather more than anyone else. He was one of the very few who had seen the leprechaun there. I was grateful to God that I was privileged to be so closely related to one who had seen the leprechaun. It wasn't a case of hearsay.

And I was grateful to God as well and equally grateful to Grandfather that they both should agree I be allowed to come to the well this fine spring day.

Wasn't it a blessed day for me.

But there was no sight of the leprechaun yet. He mightn't be up. Or maybe he hadn't returned.

Returned from where I don't know, because nobody knows where the leprechaun goes. Where so which or ever I wouldn't be a bit surprised if he'd be there today, what with the grand weather we were having.

I decided I'd send a boat across for him. No problem there. Flags were growing profusely.

And look at me now, a boat builder. A knack I had inherited from Grandfather, it would seem. Though it wasn't flag boats he made in his heyday but the real thing. However, a flag boat would do the trick fine today. I wasn't long making it and sails and all on top.

I pushed it out with a crew on board. Myself and two others. And I pretended to put Grandfather in as well and considered the other two terribly ignorant of the sails. Off we went smoothly and pleasantly — making for the harbour on the other side of the well.

The leprechaun had to be somewhere on the other side.

Now that the boat had set sail with all of us aboard I could take a breather. I was able to imagine that I had stayed ashore as well. It is a great advantage to me that I have that gift. Nothing could please me better than to be ploughing the waves and at the same time to be looking out at the boat in the middle of the bay...

I was looking at my own shadow in the water below me too. Stretching out and growing and going off in little waves forever outwards. My face smiling up at me...

The water clouded. The dog I thought. But this shadow hadn't two dog's ears. I had to leave the wonder of the well and look over my shoulder.

51

It was Máire Bhán. Come for a bucket of water. I got out of her way, without saying anything, to allow her to the water.

I had no intention of telling her anything about what was going on in the well. I let nothing on.

But she wasn't a great gabber anyway. Not that I knew her very well. How would I, but I'd heard at home that she was a bit weird. She'd rarely go out and only spoke to people the odd time.

She started filling the bucket with a saucepan.

I had my own bothers. I started calling the dog. He didn't come. I suppose he was just as happy as I was to have his way.

"Has he gone off on you?" the woman asked.

She was in talking form today, it seemed. She spoke soft and gently.

"Musha, he has," says I "the old brute," because I was an innocent chatty lad in those days.

"Oh, he'll be along. Don't worry," says she, idly. But then I saw she was peering sharply into my eyes. And then I noticed she was looking as if something strange had crossed her mind.

You'd think her face was changing. She continued talking.

"Unless he does what that playboy did on me long ago... and never come back."

"What playboy?"

"Oh make no mistake about it. Or didn't they tell you about your Uncle Martin — the greatest boyo on all these islands. He went off and left me..."

I wasn't getting her drift very well. With Grandfather I didn't have to listen if I didn't want to. I had to listen to her. But she hadn't much else to say. She appeared to snap out of it.

"O musha, it's a long while ago now, maceen. Bless the mark, be sure you don't turn out like him. Of course, you won't... with the help of God... Oh, musha, musha, I'd completely forgotten him — before he came into my head

53

a while ago. Whatever it was that brought him to mind..."

And the old woman went off with plenty to do carrying that heavy bucket. Off to the old thatched house where she lived alone — Tí Mháire Bhán.

She left me there. By myself.

The cloud she had cast over the well had gone off with her. In its place the cold venom of spring.

I noticed my boat had gone aground on the rocks and nothing to keep it steady. Rocking and crashing, this way and that... No sign of the crew. They had gone. Why wouldn't they?

Wasn't the captain more interested in talking to an old woman than looking after his vessel. I was now a captain without a crew, without a boat. And I was getting cold on shore...

I heard the dog barking, as if he had come on a rabbit. I went up the boreen to where the barking was.

He was up on the height, inside in the huge rock mound, the one they call *An Chreig Aird*. Into the mound with me. But I couldn't get a chance to figure out what he was up to because my mother was at the ditch by this time, half crazy.

I was about to tell her about all the wonders I had seen today but she put across me angrily.

"Home with you quick," says she, "or what are you thinking at all? Do you know I've walked the island looking for you, you little brat..."

She was heading for me as she was saying this. I thought it best to keep clear of her for a while. I went over the stile in a hurry. We set off for home. The dog in front. Myself behind him walking as purposefully as I could, and with good reason...

Grandfather was there when we arrived and not a bother in the world on him. He gave us a great welcome and said something to my mother "wasn't it great himself, the little man, was back..."

It was nice to see someone grand and happy.

Soon my mother was happy enough too. When she

had drank her tea she began to forget the day's goings on. But that was when I was most thinking of my adventures.

Of course what was bothering me the worst was that my boat was smashed. But there was something else that I couldn't get out of my head: Máire Bhán and her story. Uncle Martin? Where was he?

The question was barely in my head when it was in my mouth.

"Where did Uncle Martin go to?"

It was Grandfather who replied.

"Martin, is it?" says he.

"Yes, Máire Bhán was telling me about him. Where is he now?"

Grandfather took the tongs and began stirring the embers in search of a glow to redden his pipe.

"Ah, will you stop," says he rudely. "Didn't I send him out to the cow earlier on a long while and the devil a leg or a bone of him has come back yet. That's true. I'm distracted by him... trying to shove some sense into his skull."

Grandfather lit his pipe and stayed quiet.

I had to ask my mother.

"What's Grandfather saying? Wasn't it *me* he sent to the cow today?"

"Musha, don't mind Grandfather, maceen. Sure he's only raving. Old people get foolish sometimes, you see..."

"But Máire Bhán was talking about Uncle Martin as well..."

"But sure isn't *she* full of codology as well? It's no wonder, the poor woman. When you're big you'll know. Don't bother your head now with the old stories that grown ups have. Haven't you much else to be doing besides?"

It was true. I had other things to do.

I had turned the stool upside down. That was my curragh whenever I was going fishing. And my chief concern now.

Conamara: An Tír Aineoil: Bob Quinn / Liam Mac Con Iomaire
£20 (hb) ISBN 1 900693 39 9
Some of the best-known people in Conamara, the Aran Islands, and Ráth Cairn in Co Meath are captured here by Bob Quinn's camera and by Liam Mac Con Iomaire's portraits in prose.

Aran Song: John Canter
£3.99 ISBN 1 874700 88 5
Canter has the eye of a photographer, geologist, botanist, and archaeologist, and this journal—like exploration of life, death, and civilization is likely to provide compulsive reading, not only for visitors to Aran, but also for readers worldwide who ponder the eternal mystery of the workings of the human mind.

– Glór Chonamara

The Anvy: Pádraig Standún
£3.99 ISBN 1 874700 80 X
Already hailed in Irish as a great read, this is the extraordinary but totally credible tale of a strange beast that stalks an island community by night. Children have seen the 'Anvy' and say he is a a hairy, naked, harmless creature. Others are not so sure. Is he man or beast, *púca* or devil? Perhaps he doesn't exist at all? Islanders go about their daily business in a rapidly changing world, graphically and often uproariously depicted by Standún. Earthy, eerie . . . a book with a warm, pulsating heart.

Birthway: Colm Corless
£4 ISBN 1 874700 04 4
The poetry of Kinvara's Colm Corless has featured in various publications. Now, finally, his first and long-awaited collection of poems has arrived. This exploration of the simple yet extraordinary beauty of the natural world is presented from an angle laden with insight, humour, joy, darkness.

Blind Raftery: Criostoir O'Flynn
£9 ISBN 1 900 693 240
A bilingual anthology containing a selection of poems in Irish, with English translations, by the famous blind poet, Anthony Raftery from Mayo (1784-1835). Comprehensive introductory essay in English and notes on theme and background of poems.

Byzantium: W. B. Yeats. Ed. Rosenstock / Mac Eoin
£5 ISBN 1 874700 85 0
W.B. Yeats strived to Gaelicize his poetry, both thematically and structurally, believing that knowledge of the Irish language was essential to any real understanding and expression of Ireland and the Irish. Although he failed in his own efforts to learn the language, he would have undoubtedly gained much pleasure from this superb collection of some of his best verse translated into Irish.

Colainn ar Bharr Lasrach / Cuerpo En Llamas: Francisco X. Alarcón / Rosenstock
  £6   ISBN 1 900693 32 1
Original poems in Spanish by an American Chicano poet with Irish versions and an
introductory essay in English. A proper commemoration of five hundred years of white
conquest.

Exile: Pádraig Ó Conaire. Trans. Gearailt Mac Eoin.
  £7.50 ISBN 1 874700 62 1
*This important novel is more relevant now than when it first appeared eighty-five years ago . . .
Ó Conaire's real achievement is the power unleashed by his plain, naive style.*
                                                                    – *Books Ireland*

*It is a harrowing account of this exile; it is an extraordinary book; it is, to paraphrase the late John
Jordan, the objective correlative of a great spiritual wound.*
                                                                    – *Gabriel Fitzmaurice*

Facing South: Patrick Gallagher
  £5 ISBN 1 874.00 532
. . . the first collection of poetry by this eminent 61 year-old scholar . . . Facing South *reveals an
elegance, irony and fondness for rhyme that would no doubt be deemed dreadfully old-fashioned by
those who can't achieve any of these things. I got a good deal of pleasure from it.*
                                                                    – *The Irish Times*

Fourfront: Micheál Ó Conghaile, Pádraic Breathnach, Dara Ó Conaola, Alan Titley
  £7.50 ISBN 1 902420 01 2
They have been read in Croatia and in Romania. Now four of the most talented and
successful Irish-language writers are available in translation to English.
The short story has flourished as a literary form in Ireland, not least amongst Irish-
language writers. This lively anthology will be enjoyed by all and will be cherished by
those with an interest in Irish literature, those in the field of Irish Studies and those with
an interest in Translation Studies. It illustrates very diverse styles of writing and differing
approaches to translation. It is a good example of the vibrancy of Irish-language writing
today and demonstrates, in Declan Kiberd's words, 'that the example of Kafka has been as
fully assimilated as that of *Leabhar Sheáin Í Chonaill*.'

Homecoming: Cathal Ó Searcaigh
  £9 ISBN 1 874700 559
*One of our most sensitive and lyrical poets, there is a quality in some writers that is beyond artifice.
Ó Searcaigh's poetry has the stamp of genuineness beyond any well-wrought turns.*
                                                                    – *Books Ireland*

*A strong confident Northern voice. The Irish language is used here with classical precision and
assurance. He evokes the mystique of his Donegal landscape with passion and gusto . . . This is the
voice of a sophisticated contemporary craftsman.*
                                                                    – *Máire Mhac an tSaoi*

Irish Comic Poems: Criostoir O'Flynn.
  £7.50   ISBN 1 874700 33 8
*O'Flynn's book is a well-researched and captivatingly original look at the comic tradition in Irish
poetry. A treat for those who like a light read but also a treat for more serious students of verse who
wish to explore the craftsmanship and technical complexity behind the serio-comic verse of the Gaelic
word-musicians.*
                                                                    – *The Celtic Pen*

The Listowel Literary Phenomenon: Ed. Gabriel Fitzmaurice.
£7.50   ISBN 1 874700 87 7
Listowel's vast literary tradition is simply too much for most people to take in. A new 'bluffer's guide' to North Kerry literature is going to be in shops in the coming weeks and must be considered a must-buy for those with a genuine interest in the literary heritage of North Kerry. For anyone who wants to learn about the creative literary tradition of North Kerry, this is the ideal volume.
— The Kerryman

The March Hare: Pádraic Breathnach
£7.50   ISBN 1 874700 03 6
Pádraic Breathanch is representative of a generation of writers in Irish bridging two worlds. Vitriol, loneliness, blind hate, social awkwardness, guilt, self-doubt, the dreams of youth, rites of passage; Breathnach is glorious and unmatched in his depiction of decay, the decay of social, cultural and moral fabrics, of landscape and of mind gone to seed.

Measuring Angles: Fred Johnston
£3   ISBN 1 874700 117
52 poems from Belfast's Fred Johnston, with accompanying cassette. Galway-based Johnston is a multi-award winning writer, poet and journalist and initiated CÚIRT, Galway's annual poetry festival, in 1986. He received an Arts Council Bursary in Literature in 1993 and was appointed Writer in Residence to Galway Library.

Poems I Wish I'd Written: Gabriel Fitzmaurice
£6   ISBN 1 900693 14 3
Poems I Wish I'd Written gathers Gabriel Fitzmaurice's favourite translations from the above anthologies together with new translations of Cathal Buí Mac Giolla Ghunna and Raifteirí and includes his much-admired translation of 'An Phurgóid' by Micheál Ó Hairtnéide (Michael Hartnett) together with translations of Máirtín Ó Direáin, Seán Ó Ríordáin, Máire Mhac an tSaoi, Caitlín Maude, Áine Ní Ghlinn, Michael Davitt, Gabriel Rosenstock and others.

The Space Between: Gabriel Fitzmaurice
£3   ISBN 1 874700 56 7
A collection of poems. Also available on cassette.

The Village Sings: Gabriel Fitzmaurice
£6.95   ISBN1 900693 09 7
The Village Sings, Gabriel Fitzmaurice's sixth collection of poems in English for adults, celebrates life in a close, rural community in County Kerry. Beginning with politics as it emerges from the War of Independence and the foundation of the State, it traces the life of the village through the eyes of the local poet and schoolmaster. It examines the role of the teacher in his community, and follows the people as they re-create themselves in the Village Hall, the Football Field, in Church, in their use of language, their music-making, in their imagination on art, politics, family, the supernatural and village life.

Um an nGrá Dorcha/De Amor Oscuro: Francisco X. Alarcón/Gabriel Rosenstock
£6/$9   ISBN 1 900693 67 4
A heartfelt love poem with a particular insight into homosexuality.

30 Zen Haiku: J. W. Hackett / Gabriel Rosenstock
£5   ISBN 1 874700 42 7
An attractive booklet of haiku verse exhibiting close observation, verbal agility, silence.